TITCH

by PAT HUTCHINS

Aladdin Paperbacks

Aladdin Paperbacks
An imprint of Simon & Schuster
Children's Publishing Division
1230 Avenue of the Americas
New York, NY 10020
Copyright © 1971 by Pat Hutchins
First Aladdin Paperbacks edition, 1993
Printed in Hong Kong
20 19 18 17

Library of Congress Cataloging-in-Publication Data
Hutchins Pat. 1942-
    Titch / by Pat Hutchins
      p. cm.
    Summary: Titch feels left out because he is so much smaller than his
brother and sister until he gets a little seed that grows bigger than anything
they have.
    ISBN 0-689-71688-5
    [1. Size—Fiction.   2. Brothers and sisters—Fiction.]   I. Title.
PZ7H96165Ti   1993
[E]—dc20   92-1642

For Darren

Titch was little.

His sister Mary
was a bit bigger.

And his brother Pete
was a lot bigger.

Pete had a great big bike.

Mary had a big bike.

And Titch had a little tricycle.

Pete had a kite
that flew high
above the trees.

Mary had a kite
that flew high
above the houses.

And Titch had a pinwheel
that he held in his hand.

Pete had a big drum.

Mary had a trumpet.

And Titch had
a little wooden whistle.

Pete had a big saw.

Mary had a big hammer.

And Titch held the nails.

Pete had a big spade.

Mary had a fat flowerpot.

But Titch had the tiny seed.

And Titch's seed grew

and grew

and grew.